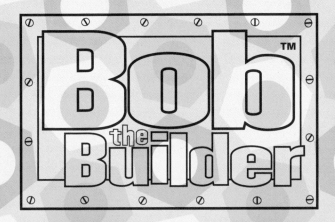

BBC CHILDREN'S BOOKS
Published by the Penguin Group
Penguin Books Ltd, 80 Strand, London WC2R 0RL, England
Penguin Group (Australia), 250 Camberwell Road, Camberwell, Victoria 3124,
Australia (a division of Pearson Australia Group Pty Ltd)
The Knights of Can-a-Lot first published by BBC Worldwide Ltd, 2003
Text and design © BBC Children's Character Books, 2003
This edition published by BBC Children's Books, 2006
Adapted by Iona Treahy based on the script by Sarah Ball and Jimmy Hibbert
Can Spud Fix It? first published by BBC Worldwide Ltd, 2000
Text and design © BBC Children's Character Books, 2000
This edition published by BBC Children's Books, 2006
Written by Diane Redmond
Bob's Bugle first published by BBC Worldwide Ltd, 1999
Text and design © BBC Children's Character Books, 1999
This edition published by BBC Children's Books, 2006
Written by Diane Redmond
Pilchard Steals the Show first published by BBC Worldwide Ltd, 2002
Text and design © BBC Children's Character Books, 2002
This edition published by BBC Children's Books, 2006
Written by Iona Treahy based on a script by Jimmy Hibbert
Scoop's Stegosaurus first published by BBC Worldwide Ltd, 2001
Text and design © BBC Children's Character Books, 2000
This edition published by BBC Children's Books, 2006
Written by Diane Redmond based on a script by Jimmy Hibbert
CBeebies & logo™ BBC. © BBC 2002
BBC & logo © and ™ BBC 1996
10 9 8 7 6 5 4 3 2 1
Based upon the television series
Bob the Builder © 2006 HIT Entertainment Ltd. and Keith Chapman.
The Bob the Builder name and character and the Wendy, Spud, Roley,
Muck, Pilchard, Dizzy, Lofty and Scoop characters are trademarks of
HIT Entertainment Ltd. Registered in the UK.
With thanks to HOT Animation
www.bobthebuilder.com
All rights reserved.
ISBN 10: 1 405 90298 1   ISBN 13: 978 1 405 90298 4
Printed in China

Five Favourite Tales

BBC
CHILDREN'S BOOKS

Contents

The Knights of Can-a-Lot

One morning, someone arrived at Bob's yard. His name was Bob, too.

"Hi, Dad," said Bob. "I didn't expect you until the summer."

"I was bored at home," explained Bob's dad.

"I need a project to do."

In the office the telephone rang and
Bob's dad answered it.

"Hello, this is Dr Mountfitchett. Castle
Camelot needs fixing. Can you help?"

"Yes, we can!" said Bob's dad.

Dr Mountfitchett came to Bob's yard and
showed Bob's dad a plan of the castle.
She thought he was Bob the Builder!

"We'll go over to Castle Camelot now
to take a look," Bob's dad said.

There was a moat around the castle, so they couldn't reach it to go inside.

"Knights – like Sir Lancelot – would lower a drawbridge over the moat to let in friends, and raise it to keep out enemies," explained Dr Mountfitchett.

"That's your first job, team," said Bob's dad. "Build a drawbridge."

"Can we build Camelot?" called Scoop.

"Yes, we can!" giggled Dizzy.

"Camelot...Can-a-lot. We can a lot!"
"Meet the knights of Can-a-lot!" laughed
Muck. "Bob's dad is Sir Boss-a-lot!"

Bob's dad decided to mend the castle gate. But then...

"Help!" he yelled. "I'm stuck!"

Bob's dad was stuck to the chains that raised and lowered the gate. Lofty had to rescue him with his hook.

To keep his dad out of trouble, Bob persuaded him to clip the maze hedges. But then…

"Help," shouted Bob's dad. "I'm lost in the maze!"

Lofty had to lift Bob high up so that he could see his dad to tell him how to get out.

A bit later, Bob was clipping some ivy when he found a hidden door.

"It's the lost door to the dungeon!" cried Dr Mountfitchett.

They pushed it open and went inside. But Bob's dad closed the door by mistake. They were trapped!

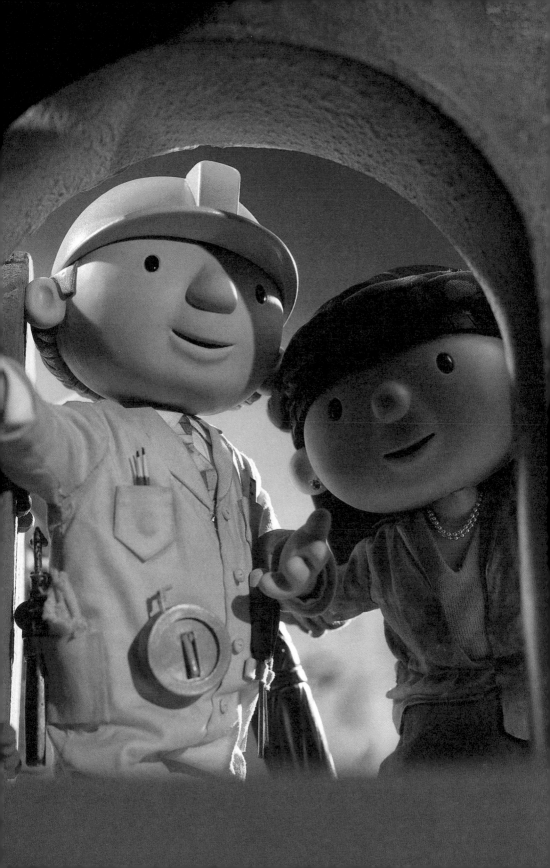

Bob's dad bravely went off to look for a way out. He fell against a wall, and it opened. He was pushed out in the maze again!

Bob's dad cut through the hedges to escape from the maze!

"Oh no!" said Bob when he saw the hedges. "They're ruined!"

Dr Mountfitchett thought the hedges looked wonderful.

"They're shaped like knights," she beamed.

When the castle was fixed, there was a grand opening with lots of visitors, including Bob's mum. Everyone had dressed up.

"Who's going to be king?" asked Dr Mountfitchett.

"You can be King, Dad," said Bob.

"No, you'd make a better king," insisted Bob's dad.

So Bob declared, "I, King of Can-a-lot, knight thee. Arise, Sir Dad-a-lot!"

THE END!

Can Spud Fix It?

It was early morning in Bob's Building Yard.
Bob was getting ready to go to the pond
and put up a new sign.

"Here's your toolbox," said Wendy, as she passed him the heavy box.

Bob climbed aboard Scoop. "Let's go," he said leading Lofty and Dizzy out of the yard.

Down the road, Spud was complaining
to Travis.

"Being a scarecrow isn't as easy as you
think," he grumbled.

Suddenly the old gate that he was leaning
against gave way and Spud fell over.

"Right, that's it!" said Spud crossly. "I'm going to get a new job. I could be a pilot!"

"You can't fly!" laughed Travis.

"I could learn," insisted Spud. Spreading his arms like aeroplane wings, he flapped them up and down.

Just then, Bob and the machines came chugging around the corner and almost crashed into Spud.

"Look out!" yelled Bob. Scoop slammed on his brakes sending Bob's toolbox flying.

"Spud! You should never play near roads! Now, please go and tell Farmer Pickles that I won't be able to fix the window frames in the old cottage until tomorrow. Thank you," cried Bob, as he headed off to the pond.

"Yes, Bob. Sorry, Bob," muttered Spud.

Spud saw Bob's toolbox on the road.

"Forget Spud the Scarecrow!" he cried as he pulled out a bright shiny spanner. "From now on I'm Spud the Spanner! I'm going to be a builder just like Bob!"

Then Spud pulled out a hammer and started to mend the gate. "This building stuff is easy!" he giggled. "I think I'll go and fix the cottage windows next."

When Bob got to the duck pond he discovered that his toolbox was missing.

"My favourite spanner is in it," he moaned.

Bob asked Lofty to go back and see if the toolbox had fallen out during the journey.

As Lofty was looking for Bob's toolbox, he bumped into Spud, who was carrying the toolbox.

"Er, Spud," Lofty said nervously, "that's Bob's toolbox. Can I have it back, please?"

"Only if you help me with a bit of building first," said Spud.

Lofty didn't really like the idea but he agreed to help.

"Hurray!" yelled Spud. "I've got a machine. Now I'm a proper builder!"

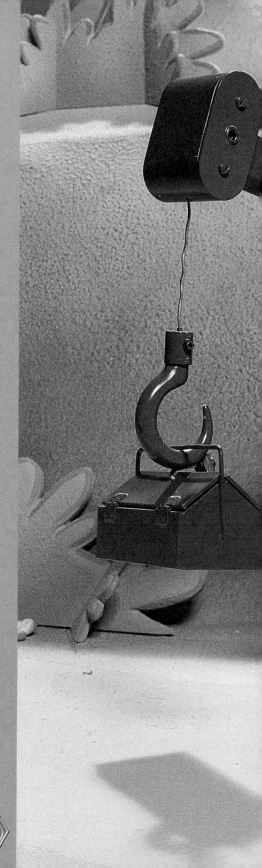

At the pond Bob waited and waited for
Lofty. He decided to phone Wendy to get her
to send Muck over with his spare toolbox.

On his way over, Muck bumped into Lofty
and Spud.

"We're off to fix the cottage windows,"
shouted Spud, as they sped past.

Muck rushed to the pond.

"Bob! Bob!" Muck cried. "Lofty and Spud are on their way to the old cottage with your toolbox!"

"Let's go team!" said Bob. "We've got to stop Spud before he hurts himself."

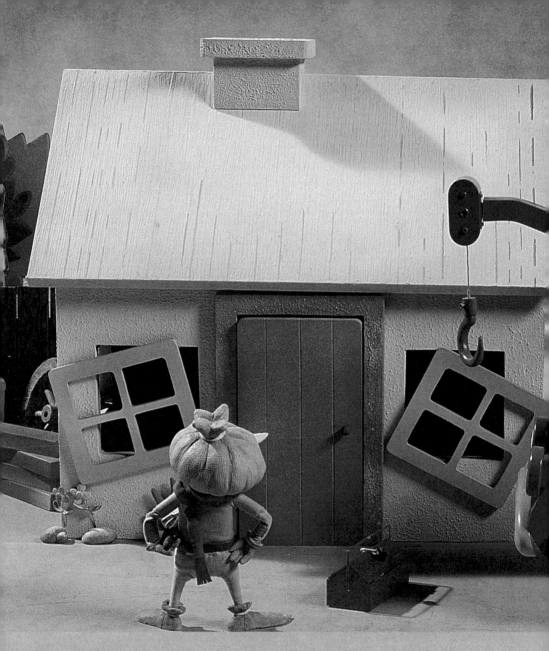

At the old cottage, Spud admired the work he had done. "Not a bad job!" he said proudly.

Lofty clanked nervously. "Oh, er, but... erm... all the windows are crooked!"

"That's how they're supposed to look!" laughed Spud. "Come on Lofty. One of the barns has a bit of the roof missing and we're going to fix it!"

"Oh no!" whimpered Lofty.

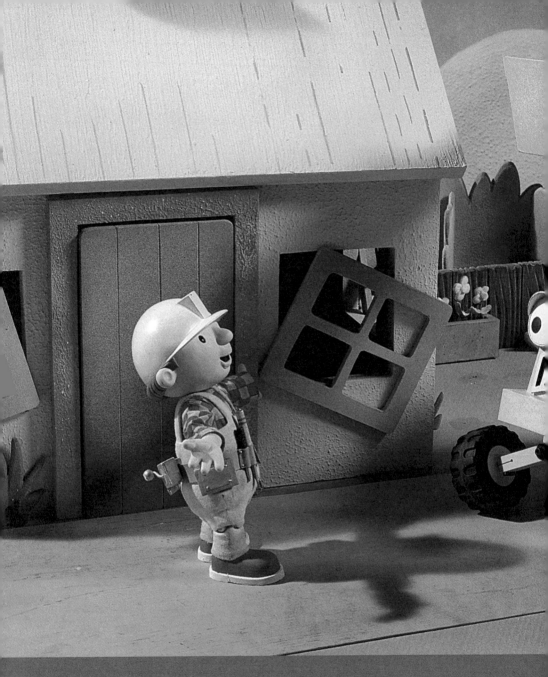

Bob, Scoop, Muck and Dizzy arrived at the old cottage. They couldn't believe their eyes when they saw the mess Spud had made.

"Oh, no!" cried Bob. "We'd better sort the windows out before there is an accident."

At the barn Spud strapped a sheet of roofing onto his back, and got Lofty to lift him up onto the roof.

"This is exciting," he said.

"Please be careful, Spud!" pleaded Lofty.

"Don't you worry," laughed Spud. "This is a job for Spud the Spanner!"

Just then a huge gust of wind blew him off the roof! Spud sailed through the air.

"H-E-L-P!" cried Spud as the wind blew him on.

Back at the old cottage, Muck looked up at the sky.

"What's that?" he wondered.

"Wow!" Dizzy squeaked excitedly. "It looks like a flying Spud!"

They all stared up at Spud who was flying straight towards them.

"Whey! Arrrghh!" Spud cried as he landed on the chimney of the old cottage.

"Nice landing, Spud," chuckled Bob.

Bob said he would only get Spud down if he promised never to use his tools again.

"Ummm, I'm sorry, Bob," mumbled Spud.

"And where's my toolbox?" asked Bob.

"Er, it's all right, Bob. I've got it," said Lofty as he came clanking up.

"Thank you, Lofty," said Bob. "Now you can get Spud down."

Lofty gently lowered Spud to the ground.

"I think I'll stay a scarecrow," Spud said. "It's much safer than being a builder!"

THE END!

Bob's Bugle

Bob was busy mending a broken central heating system. Muck was helping him.

"Now that the hot water tank is fitted, it's time to check the pipes!" Bob explained to Muck.

One of the pipes was blocked by a little bit of dirt. Bob blew down the pipe and the dirt popped out.

Bleurgh-boo-boo-bloooh! whistled the pipe, as Bob blew through it.

"Listen to this, Muck!" laughed Bob, and he blew again.

T-o-o-o -t-tee-tooooooot-tooooooot!

"What is it... a frog with a sore throat?" Muck asked.

"No!" said Bob, excitedly. "It's my bugle! Or it will be, when I've finished making it!"

"What's a bugle?" Muck asked.

"It's a musical instrument," Bob explained. "You blow in one end and a loud noise comes out of the other end."

Back at the yard, Wendy was staring into space, looking thoughtful.

"What are you thinking about?" asked Scoop.

"Some friends of mine have moved to a
new house and I want to buy them a gift, but
I can't think what to get!" answered Wendy.

Muck and Bob roared into the yard. Bob
hurried into his workshop and shut the door.

The machines and Wendy clustered outside. They could hear strange bangs and clanks. Suddenly, a loud parp! made them jump. Bob came out of his workshop, waving his shiny new bugle.

"What's that awful noise?" cried Wendy.

"Shhh Wendy," whispered Muck. "It's Bob's new bugle, and he thinks it's great!"

"So do I!" rumbled Roley.

"Perhaps I could join a band!" chuckled Bob loudly.

"You'll have to practise if you want to be in a band," said Roley.

"You're right," agreed Bob.

"Can I practise? Yes I can!"

Bob practised his bugle all night long.
Bloo-hoo-doo-diddley-doo!

"I want to go to sleep!" wailed Scoop.

"Shall we, er… tell Bob we don't like it…?" Lofty wondered.

"Hey, come on!" rumbled Roley. "Bob's having fun!"

The tired machines listened as the bugle blasts slowly turned to weak toot-toots then one last paaarp.

"At last! He's stopped!" gasped Scoop.

The next morning, Wendy was still trying to think of a present for her friends.

"I hardly slept last night, worrying about it," she said.

"We hardly slept last night because of Bob playing his bugle!" grumbled Muck.

Just then, Bob came into the yard, playing his bugle.

"Come on, Muck!" Bob called. "We've got work to do." And as he walked into his workshop, he carefully put his bugle by the door.

"Now's our chance, Lofty! Grab the bugle!" said Scoop.

Lofty extended his crane and hooked the bugle onto it.

"Put it on the roof. Bob will never find it there!" said Dizzy.

Carefully, Lofty put the bugle on the roof.

But then Bird hopped over to the bugle and started to push it with his beak.

"Oh no!" cried Muck as the bugle rolled off the roof into his scoop.

"What was that?" called Bob.

"Nothing!" said Muck.

"Come on, Muck. We've got to finish that central heating job!" said Bob.

While Bob packed his tools, Muck looked for somewhere to hide the bugle. Dizzy ran up to him and tipped her mixer forwards.

"Stick it in here," she whispered.
But then disaster struck!
"I'll need you too, Dizzy!" called Bob.
"Me! Why?" she said nervously.
"To mix concrete, of course!" said Bob.

At the house, Bob went inside to fix the radiators.

"Ding-a-dong-a-ding!" he sang, as he tapped the radiators with his hammer.

"Nice music, but not as good as my bugle!" Bob said.

Outside, Dizzy and Muck wondered what to do with the bugle.

Suddenly, Bob appeared at the door with a bucket.

"Cement please Dizzy!" he said

"Are you sure?" gulped Dizzy.

"Here goes…" sighed Dizzy. She poured the cement into Bob's bucket.

Glug-glug-glug-CLANG! Bob's bugle, covered in cement, fell into the bucket.

"How did that get there?" Bob cried with disbelief.

"No idea!" mumbled Muck and Dizzy.

"Never mind – I'll soon have it cleaned up," smiled Bob.

Back at the yard, Bob cleaned his dirty bugle carefully. Then he gently put it on the ground.

"Roley, can you help me over here for a minute?" called Bob.

"Ok, Bob," rumbled Roley.

As he rolled forwards there was a terrible crunch! Roley had squashed Bob's bugle!

"Oh, no! I'm so sorry Bob!" cried Roley.

Bob could see that Roley was upset.

"Don't worry. I shouldn't have left it on the ground," sighed Bob. As he picked up the flattened bugle, the broken pieces went tinkle, tinkle.

"That's a lovely set of wind chimes," said Wendy, coming out of her office. "Just the sort of present I've been looking for!"

"There I was, thinking I'd made a bugle, when it was really a set of wind chimes!" smiled Bob. "You can have these for your friends, Wendy."

"Thanks, Bob," cried Wendy, shaking the chimes.

Tinkle, tinkle, tinkle!

"Ah..." sighed Scoop happily. "Nice, quiet wind chimes..."

"I quite liked the bugle myself!" rumbled Roley.

THE END!

Pilchard Steals
the Show

Bob and the machines were building a barn for Farmer Pickles's sheep.

"Can we fix it?" Scoop called to everyone.

"Yes, we can!" the other machines replied.

Roley made the ground nice and smooth, ready for the barn to stand on.

As they were working, Bob heard a whistling sound. The sound came again, and Bob spotted Farmer Pickles on the other side of the hedge.

Farmer Pickles was training Scruffty to sit, walk and roll over.

"That's really good. Well done, you two!" called Bob.

"I have high hopes for Scruffty winning the dog show today," said Farmer Pickles.

"Hey, Bob!" said Scoop. "How about entering Pilchard in the show? She's just as smart as Scruffty – I bet she could win."

"I'm sorry Scoop, but it's a dog show – no cats allowed," chuckled Farmer Pickles.

"Oh well, never mind Scoop," said Bob.

Scoop, however, was determined to enter the show with Pilchard. He went back to the yard to look for her.

"Pilchard!" he called. "Pil-chaaard, come!"

Pilchard came out, wondering what all the noise was about.

"There, see?" said Scoop. "You came when I called you. It is going to be easy-peasy to train you. What do you think, Pilchard?"

"Miaow!" cried Pilchard.

Scoop tried whistling at Pilchard, but
the noise only frightened her. But he wasn't
giving up on his plan to enter the show.
Eventually, he persuaded Pilchard to sit in his
scoop, and off they went to the dog show.

When they got to the enclosure, Pilchard spotted a mouse and shot straight past Scoop, after it.

"Pilchard! Come back!" cried Scoop. "We don't have much time before the show starts."

Pilchard turned and walked towards Scoop, leaving the mouse to escape.

"Good Pilchard!" said Scoop. But as he moved forward he got tangled in the flags around the enclosure.

"Oh no!" squealed Scoop. "Help, Pilchard! I'm stuck!"

Pilchard ran to Farmer Pickles's farm to get some help.

Bob and the team were just finishing putting the roof on the new barn. Pilchard tried to get Wendy's attention by rubbing up against her leg.

"Miaow!" cried Pilchard loudly and stuck out her paw.

"Er – I think she wants us to follow her," said Wendy.

"Let's go!" said Bob, and they set off after Pilchard.

Pilchard raced ahead, and led them
to Scoop.

"Well done, Pilchard!" said Scoop with
a big smile on his face.

"Can we fix it?" said Bob.

"Yes, we can!" shouted the others, as Lofty pulled the flags off Scoop.

"Thanks, everyone!" said Scoop. "And you know something," he said to Pilchard. "If they did let cats enter dog shows, you'd be the winner for sure."

Bob asked Mrs Percival, who was one of the judges, if it would be all right for a cat to enter a dog show.

"It's a most unusual request, Bob," said Mrs Percival. "But it may be possible. I'll see what I can do."

A little while later the show started. Farmer Pickles and Scruffty were the first to take part. Scruffty performed perfectly.

After all the dogs had been in the ring,
Mrs Percival announced Scoop and Pilchard
– the first ever cat to enter.

"Thanks, Mrs Percival," whispered Scoop.
He gently tipped Pilchard onto the grass and
gave her instructions.

The judges watched very carefully.

Pilchard walked forwards, sat down and even rolled over. And to everyone's amazement, including Scoop's, she finished off with a fancy back flip. The audience clapped and cheered.

"You have a very talented cat there, Bob," admired Farmer Pickles.

"And you have a very talented dog, too," replied Bob.

But Scruffty covered his eyes and wimpered. He knew he didn't have a chance of winning now.

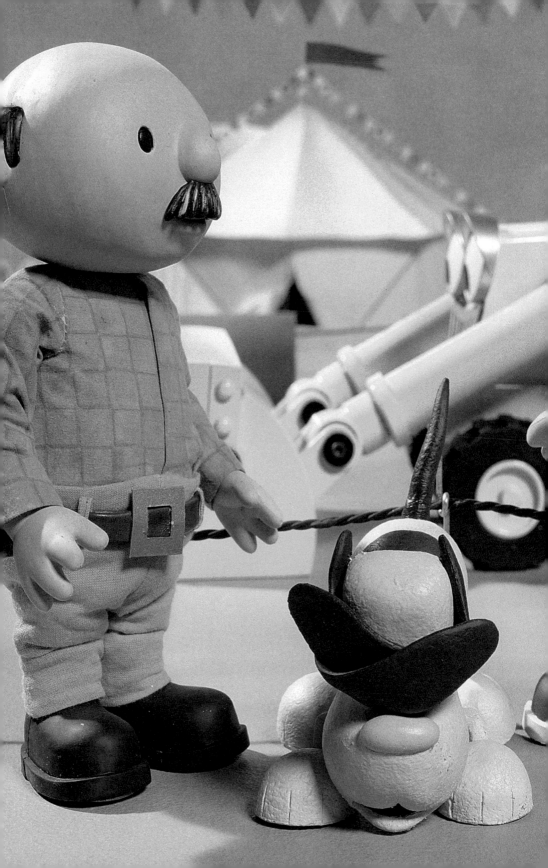

While the judges were making their
decision, Bob and the team went to
congratulate Pilchard and Scoop.

"That was brilliant, Pilchard!" said Scoop.

"Miaow!" purred Pilchard.

"If I hadn't seen it with my own eyes I would never have believed Pilchard could do all of those tricks," said Bob.

Everyone lined up for the prize-giving ceremony. There was silence as Mrs Percival carried over a trophy for the winner.

"I'm pleased to announce that the winners of this year's dog show are... Scoop and Pilchard! Well done!" said Mrs Percival.

Bob, Wendy and the machines all cheered, and Scruffty wagged his tail. Scoop felt very proud when Mrs Percival placed the trophy in Pilchard's paws.

"Miaow!" cried Pilchard happily.

THE END!

Scoop's Stegosaurus

It was a busy morning at the yard. Bob, Scoop and Lofty were off to Farmer Pickles's farm to lay some new pipes. Wendy was going into town to build some cabinets for the museum.

"Oh, Wendy, I've never seen a museum," said Dizzy. "Can I come too, pleeease?"

Wendy smiled. "Of course!" she said.

"Yesss!" Dizzy said, spinning round and round. "Thanks, Wendy!"

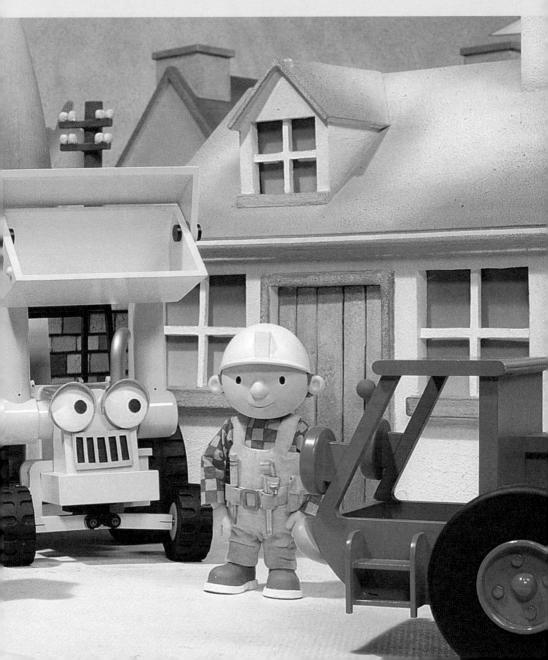

Bob, Scoop and Lofty found Farmer Pickles
looking very gloomy.

"All this rain has made my field so muddy
nothing will grow in it," he said.

"Don't worry Farmer Pickles, these pipes will drain the water off the field in no time," said Bob cheerfully.

In the museum Wendy was busy measuring the display cabinets.

Dizzy was talking to Mr Ellis, the museum curator.

"See this," he said, holding up a pot.

"It's all old and cracked," said Dizzy.

"That's because it's over four thousand years old," Mr Ellis replied. "And that means people have been living around here for ages!"

"Wow!" gasped Dizzy in amazement.

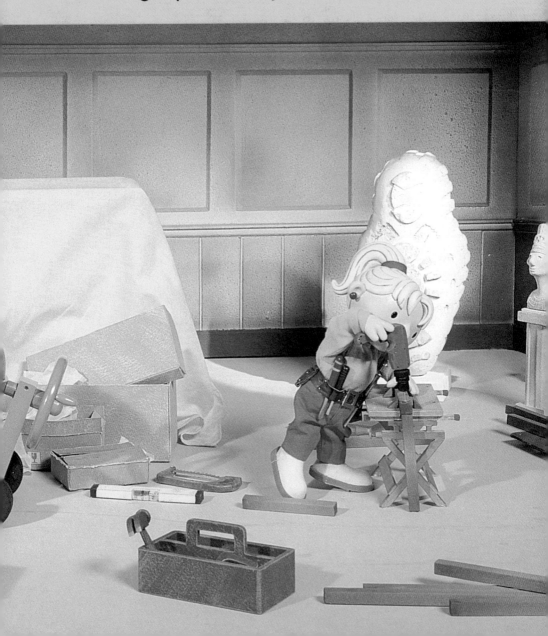

At Farmer Pickles's farm, Scoop was busy digging a deep trench when Bob spotted something.

"Hang on, Scoop! Look at these huge bones!" Bob shouted.

"Wow!" cried Scoop.

"Maybe they're dinosaur bones!" said Bob excitedly. "I'm going to ring the museum and get Mr Ellis to have a look."

Mr Ellis carefully examined all the bones in the trench.

"Scoop, you've dug up a dinosaur called a stegosaurus! I think this is a complete skeleton," he said.

"Wow!" cried Scoop and Bob.

"These bones are very old and fragile," explained Mr Ellis. "I'll have to get a special machine to collect them."

"You go, Mr Ellis. I'll guard the bones," said Scoop.

Bob covered the bones with a tarpaulin and left with Mr Ellis.

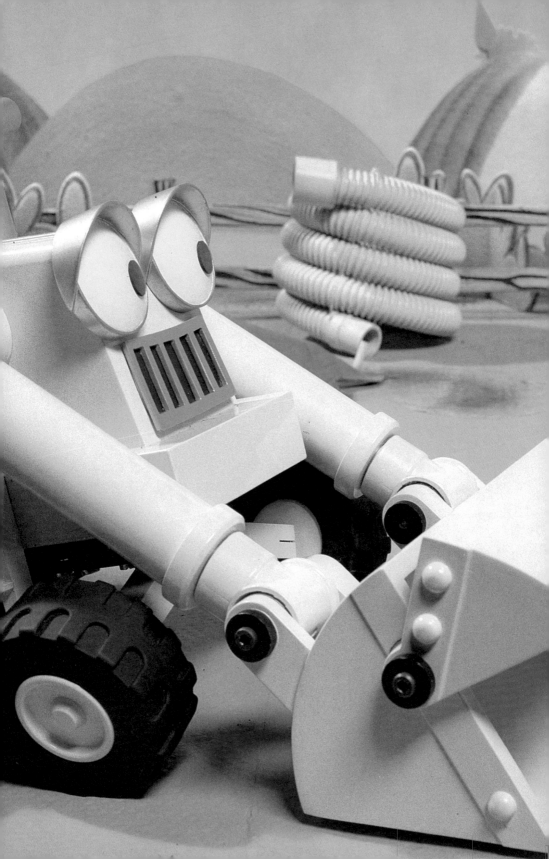

"Ooh, what's under there, Scoop?" asked Spud poking at the tarpaulin.

"I've just dug up some dinosaur bones and I'm guarding them. Nobody's allowed to see them," said Scoop firmly.

"I've found some bones, too," said Spud with a cheeky grin. "I'll let you see mine if you let me see yours."

"Oh, OK then," Scoop said and went over to the next field to take a quick look.

"Hee, hee, hee!" giggled Spud. "Cor! I'll borrow some of these bones!"

When the bones arrived at the museum, Mr Ellis studied the plan he had made.

"That's strange," he said to Bob. "There are bones missing. If we had a complete skeleton, our little museum would have been famous all over the world."

"What a shame," said Bob. "Maybe there are still some bones left in the field?"

Bob didn't find any other bones in the field.

"Maybe the missing bones are the ones Spud found?" said Scoop thoughtfully.

"Spud?" gasped Bob.

"Yes, Spud told me he'd found some bones in the next field, but I couldn't find them. I was only away a few minutes," said Scoop.

"Oh, no! I think I know who has got our missing bones!" said Bob as he hurried off.

Meanwhile...

"Roll up! Roll up! Come and see
SPUDULOSAURUS, the scariest dinosaur
ever!" Spud called proudly to Travis.

"It looks like a lot of old bones to me!"
muttered Travis.

Then Bob arrived. "Spud! You found those bones under my tarpaulin sheet, didn't you?"

"Er... yes. Sorry, Bob," muttered Spud.

"They're not yours!" said Bob sternly. "I'll take them back to the museum now."

At the museum, Mr Ellis fixed all the dinosaur bones into place.

"This is magnificent!" he said proudly. "A complete stegosaurus skeleton!"

"Who would have thought that dinosaurs used to live around here?" gasped Wendy.

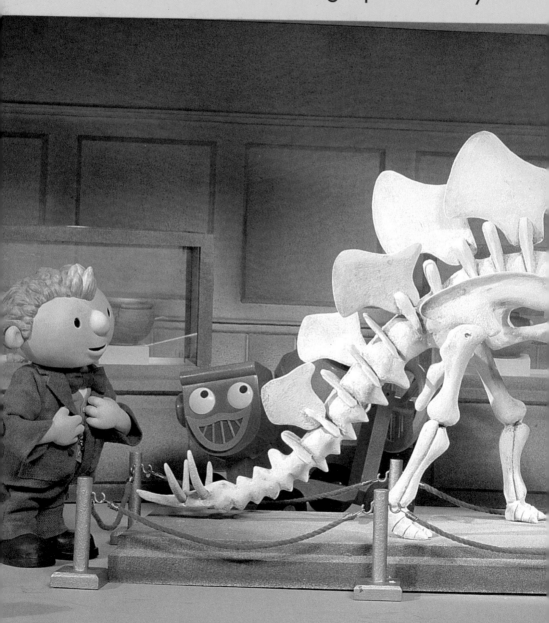

"I'm so glad they don't now," giggled Dizzy.

Mr Ellis gave Bob a present for Scoop, to say thank you for finding the dinosaur bones.

Back at the yard, Bob gave Scoop the present from Mr Ellis.

"Look!" cried Bob. "It's a toy stegosaurus."

"That's brilliant!" said Scoop proudly.

Suddenly the stegosaurus slipped out of Bob's fingers and landed on Pilchard's nose! She howled and ran across the yard.

"If Pilchard's frightened of that, just think what she'd be like if she met a Dizzyosaurus!" giggled Dizzy. "Raarghhh!"

The machines raced around the yard pretending to be big scary dinosaurs.

"Hee, hee! I'm a Scooplodicus! Grrr, grrr!" laughed Scoop.

"Look out!" called Roley. "Here comes the Roleydactyl! Ark! Ark!"

"Oooohh, I don't like dinosaurs!" cried Lofty.

"I'll save you, Lofty!" yelled Muck. "I'm the mighty Muckasaurus Rex! Raaargh!"

THE END!